Rhymes
to
Read

The Fastest Truck

by Sally Prue

Illustrated by Rory Walker

W

FRANKLIN WATTS

LONDON•SYDNEY

About this book

Rhymes to Read are designed for children who are ready to start reading alone. They can also be used by an adult to share with a child.

The books provide excellent support for developing phonological awareness, helping the child to recognise sounds and sound-symbol relationships. The poems are perfect to read aloud and the strong rhythms, rhymes and repetition will help build confidence and encourage reading and rereading for pleasure.

Reading tips for adults sharing the book with a child:

1. Make reading fun! Choose a time to read when you and the child are relaxed and have time to share the story.
2. Talk about the story before you start reading. Look at the cover and the blurb. What might the story be about? Why might the child like it?
3. Encourage the child to retell the story, using the pictures and rhymes to help. The puzzles at the back of the book provide a good starting point.
4. Give praise! Remember that small mistakes need not always be corrected.
5. For an extra activity, you could ask the child to make up some alternative rhymes for the story or their own brand new rhyme!

Tim the truck is big and green.

He's strong and fast and very mean.

He never waits.

He never stops.

4

He speeds past all
the trees and shops.

He'll race along
the smallest streets,

without a care

for those he meets.

He'll push past
anybody small,

for Tim the truck's
not nice at all.

For Tim is big and
Tim is mean,

the fastest truck

you've ever seen.

But one day Tim
ran out of luck.

He ended up
in lots of muck!

"Oh help!" he called,
"I'm sinking down.

This mud is deep,
I'm going to drown!"

"But we don't like you,
Tim the truck.

It's best for us

when you are stuck."

16

"Oh, I'll be good,"
said Tim, in fear.
"Just come and
get me out of here!"

19

So they were kind,
and got him free.
And now Tim's as

good as he can be,

at least while all

his friends can see!

Puzzle 1

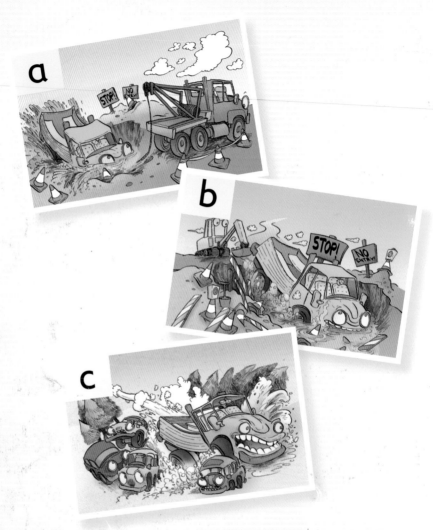

Put the pictures in the correct order and retell the story.

Puzzle 2

down
sink
deep
drown

a

b

big
mean
truck
green

Find the rhyming words above.

Turn over for answers!

Answers

Puzzle 1

The correct order is: c, b, a.

Puzzle 2

The rhyming words are:

a. down, drown

b. green, mean

First published in 2011 by
Franklin Watts
338 Euston Road
London
NW1 3BH

Franklin Watts Australia
Level 17/207 Kent Street
Sydney
NSW 2000

Text © Sally Prue 2011
Illustration © Rory Walker 2011

The rights of Sally Prue to be
identified as the author and Rory Walker
as the illustrator of this Work have been
asserted in accordance with the Copyright,
Designs and Patents Act, 1988.

A CIP catalogue record for this book is
available from the British Library.

ISBN 978 1 4451 0294 8 (hbk)
ISBN 978 1 4451 0300 6 (pbk)

Series Editor: Melanie Palmer
Series Advisor: Catherine Glavina
Series Designer: Peter Scoulding

Printed in China

Franklin Watts is a division of Hachette Children's Books,
an Hachette UK company. www.hachette.co.uk